Artemus Flint: Detective

Beryl Goldsweig

SCHOLASTIC BOOK SERVICES
New York Toronto London Auckland Sydney Tokyo

Copyright © 1974 by Beryl Goldsweig. All rights reserved. Published by Scholastic Book Services, a division of Scholastic Magazines, Inc.

1st printing . . . . October 1974
Printed in the U. S. A.

TABLE OF CONTENTS

The Case of . . .

The Case of . . .

The Alarming Accident

"Where were you at three twenty yesterday afternoon, Mrs. Derby?" Detective Artemus Flint asked the nervous-looking woman standing at the door of her home.

"I? Why, I . . . why do you want to know?" she asked.

"At three twenty someone turned in a false fire alarm," Detective Flint explained. "The alarm was sent from this street. So a lot of policemen have been going from door to door asking people where they were yesterday afternoon and whether they noticed anyone near the fire-alarm box. I'm working along with them."

"Why did the police send so many men? Surely they've got better things to do, like fighting serious crimes," snapped the woman.

"This *is* a serious crime," Flint informed her. "You see," he said, looking her in the eye, "a man is in the hospital because of that false alarm."

Mrs. Derby flinched. "The hospital? What happened?"

"In the heavy fog, one of the fire trucks answering the alarm crashed into a lamp post near your home. The driver was injured badly." Flint paused to let his words sink in. Then he said, "Now that you realize

1

what a serious crime was committed, Mrs. Derby, I'll ask you again: Where were you at three twenty yesterday afternoon?"

"Goodness," she muttered, "you act as if *I'd* done something wrong. It's all very simple really. I was driving home from the beauty parlor. As I sat in my car at the corner of Seventh and Washington Streets, waiting for the light to change, I happened to look down the street. I noticed that the Kwality Supermarket on Sixth was having a sale on apples. They had an ad in their window. So I drove there and looked at the apples. But I didn't like the way they looked, so I drove right home. I got home at three thirty, in time for my favorite soap opera."

"Did anyone see you in the supermarket?" Flint asked.

"I don't suppose so. I didn't talk to anyone." Then Mrs. Derby asked angrily, "Why are you so suspicious of *me*?"

"Because," said Flint slowly, "one of your neighbors thought she saw you near the fire-alarm box at about three twenty yesterday." He stopped, then continued. "And because," said Flint, *"your story is a lie!"*

HOW DID DETECTIVE ARTEMUS FLINT KNOW MRS. DERBY WAS LYING?

Mrs. Derby claimed she read the ad about the sale of apples down the street, on Sixth, a block away. She couldn't have *in the heavy fog* — when the driver of the fire truck couldn't even see the lamp post immediately in front of him.

The Case of . . .

The Animal-Lover's Will

Old Joseph Ringer had loved animals. He had kept a great many pets and farm animals — including an old goat named Artemus, after his friend, Detective Flint.

After Ringer died, his will was read. Ringer left $2500 to be given to a scientist to study animals. Ringer's son, Joseph, Junior, or Joe, asked Flint to be present when he interviewed the people who came to the house seeking the prize.

One by one they came in and told Joe and Flint what they would do with the money if it were awarded to them.

"I would study the deer, one of nature's most beautiful and remarkable creatures," said Professor Houghton.

"Bees interest me," said Mrs. Swain. "There is much to learn about their social order and their means of communicating with one another."

Mr. Leeward wanted to study bats. "I have studied birds for many years," he explained, "and I have always found the bat the most fascinating bird of all."

Others who were interviewed and the subjects they wanted to study were as follows:

Miss Wiley — The training of fleas.

Mr. Tell — The mating habits of female mules.

Mrs. Washburn — The intelligence of tree-dwelling monkeys.

Mr. DeLow — The flying patterns of certain species of geese.

After having interviewed all of these people, Joe turned to Flint and said, "All of those people seemed to be well-qualified. How are we ever going to decide who should get that $2500?"

"We can start," said Flint, "*by eliminating the two who are not really scientists at all.*"

WHICH TWO PEOPLE DID FLINT MEAN? HOW DID HE KNOW THAT THEY WERE NOT REALLY SCIENTISTS?

Flint knew that Mr. Leeward and Mr. Tell were not really scientists. Mr. Leeward said, "I have studied birds for many years, and I have always found the bat the most fascinating bird of all." Actually the bat is not a bird, but a mammal. Mr. Tell wanted to study "the mating habits of female mules." There is no such thing as a female mule; mules are neuter. A mule is the offspring of a horse and a donkey.

The Case of . . .

The Bashed Blonde

Flint was in Ned O'Keefe's den when he heard the screams. "Murder! Murder! Help!" a woman's voice cried out in terror. At once he was on his feet, running out the door in the direction of the screams, with Ned at his heels. Others in the neighborhood had been alerted by the screams, for a number of people were running, as Flint was, toward the house across the street from the O'Keefes', a large, impressive Tudor dwelling that obviously belonged to someone of means.

In the doorway stood a stubby woman, her face chalk white — the source of the screams. The crowd pushed past her into the living room and stared in horror at what was before them. There was the body of a blonde, early middle-aged woman lying crumpled on the floor. A brass lamp lay on the floor near her, presumably the murder weapon.

"Bashed on the head, how awful," breathed Mr. Sobel, a neighbor of Ned's whom Flint had met once or twice.

"There are no signs of a struggle," observed a man in a gray hat. "She must have been hit from behind, taken quite by surprise."

"I found her when I came in to clean the house this morning," sputtered the stubby woman. "Such a shock!"

Flint seized control of the situation. Although he hated the grim circumstances, he had to admit to himself that he enjoyed rounding up a roomful of frenzied people and using his commanding personality to whip them into an orderly assemblage that he could approach with reason. This he did.

Those present, according to Ned, were Miss Braddock, the maid, and Mr. Sobel, Mrs. Lucia, Mr. Wright, Miss Weinstein, and young Trudy Axley — all residents of the street. There were two other persons, whom Ned did not know — the man in the gray hat, and a teenage boy in a torn T-shirt. How could they account for their presence near the murdered woman's home? Flint asked them.

"I came by to ask if I could cut the grass," the boy replied in nasal tones. "I'm looking to make some extra money mowing lawns in my free time."

"I am selling encyclopedias," the man in the gray hat explained.

"I just can't get over it," Mrs. Lucia remarked then. "She was kind of eccentric, and maybe a little bit mean, but those aren't motives for murder."

"Why would anyone want to kill her?" Mr. Wright asked no one in particular.

"She used to scream at the kids a lot," Trudy volunteered. "We used to say we'd 'get her someday,' but of course we didn't mean it. We were really scared of her."

"I've never been in this neighborhood before today," the man in the gray hat said, "but it seems like a quiet, pleasant area — not a place you'd expect a murder to take place in."

"And such a grisly murder too!" Miss Weinstein

said. "I won't feel safe until the murderer is behind bars. After all, you never know when he might sneak up behind *you*!"

"Look, can I leave?" the teenage boy asked Flint. "I haven't got time — "

"Yes, we *are* wasting valuable time," the man in the gray hat interrupted. To Flint he said, "The police should be summoned immediately. I'll just run down to the phone booth I noticed at the corner and phone them."

As he got up to go, Flint placed a restraining hand on his shoulder.

"No you don't," he said firmly. "I want to make sure you're here when the police arrive — because *you're the number one suspect!*"

WHY DID DETECTIVE ARTEMUS FLINT SUSPECT THE MAN IN THE GRAY HAT?

Anyone wanting to call the police to report a murder would certainly look for the phone nearest at hand, and a stranger would assume that a wealthy woman such as the victim had a telephone in her home. However, the murdered woman was a rich eccentric who had no telephone. If the man in the gray hat had really been a stranger to the neighborhood, he would have suggested the call be made from a phone in the victim's home. He would not have suggested phoning from a phone booth unless he had known that the victim herself had no telephone in her house. Flint suspected that the man had looked for a telephone and found none when he was in the house — when he had committed the murder!

7

The Case of . . .

The Beautiful Birds

"Your wife called me," Flint told Lester Avell. "She was very worried. She said you had taken your life-savings and invested them in some stupid deal."

"She's all wrong, Art," Lester replied. "I'm going to make a fortune. My wife and I will be rich! I've gone into business with my friend Dusty — the best friend a man ever had."

"What sort of business?" asked Flint.

"Breeding peacocks. Dusty has the know-how, and I'm putting up the money. It's a great deal. I've worked hard and pinched pennies all my life, and now I'm finally going to make some big money."

"Just how well do you know this Dusty?" Artemus Flint asked.

"I've met him a couple of times. But he's a prince — a marvelous man. Want to meet him? We'll drop by his room."

Flint went with Lester to a cheap hotel. They walked up two flights of stairs and to the end of a dim hallway. At their knock Dusty, a short man with beady eyes, opened the door and invited them in.

"Lester tells me you and he are going into the business of breeding peacocks," Flint said.

"That's right," Dusty said.

"What makes you think you'll succeed? After all,

8

Lester is trusting you with all the money he's got." Flint told him.

"Oh, there's no risk," Dusty replied. "I know all there is to know about the business of raising and breeding peacocks. I bought a pair of the most beautiful peacocks. The female peacock has a beautiful green and gold train, with long feathers that have blue-green tips. The male is just as beautiful. The offspring of those two birds will bring a terrific price. We'll sell some and breed the rest. Before long, we'll have a big business."

Lester and Flint left.

"So you see, Art," Lester said, "I've put my nest egg to good use."

"No, Lester — it's a birdbrained scheme," replied Artemus Flint. *"Dusty is a swindler."*

HOW DID ARTEMUS FLINT KNOW?

Dusty said, "The female peacock has a beautiful green and gold train, with long feathers that have blue-green tips." Technically, only the male is the peacock; the female is the peahen. Furthermore, only the male has beautifully colored feathers and a train. The female has more drab coloring and no train. Lester claimed to know all about peacocks, but obviously knew little. He lied in order to swindle Lester out of his life's savings.

The Case of . . .

The Bludgeoned Body

Blood dripped profusely from the top of Farley Morgan's head, where the bludgeon had struck, and formed an ever-widening blotch on the rug. Around his prone body stood his fiancée, his stepbrother, two policemen, and Detective Artemus Flint.

Flint cleared his throat. "Now let me get this straight," he began. "You, Mr. Wadsworth, were the first to find the body."

"That's right," the wiry little man replied. "My stepbrother — that's Farley Morgan here — and I saw each other infrequently, but for some reason he wanted to see me last night. He wrote me last week that he would be in town and asked me to come to his hotel room last night. I never learned why he wanted to see me. At ten o'clock I went to his room and knocked on the door. Receiving no answer, I tried the door, and finding it unlocked, I entered. I discovered Farley lying here — exactly as you see him now."

Those assembled had previously avoided focusing their gaze on the corpse, but at Mr. Wadsworth's words their eyes shifted involuntarily to the body before them.

"Why did it take you twenty-one hours before you reported your stepbrother's murder?" asked Flint.

"I guess I was in a state of shock," the wiry little man replied. "I couldn't react. I saw that Farley was dead, and I was afraid."

"Afraid?" sniffed Morgan's fiancée Jean. "Afraid of what?"

"Afraid of what would happen. To me, I mean."

"You're not making yourself clear, Mr. Wadsworth," Flint intervened.

"You see," Wadsworth explained, "I had a motive — a very powerful motive — for killing Farley. One hundred and fifty thousand dollars!" Those assembled drew in their breath.

"I didn't kill him, of course," Wadsworth put in quickly. "But because of his death I'm a rich man. Farley's father had a great deal of money. Soon after my mother married him, she died. He made out a will leaving his entire fortune to Farley, and if Farley died without having had any children, the money was to go to me. All of it."

He shook his head sadly. "I know I shouldn't have kept silent when I discovered the murder. But I was sure you'd think I was the murderer. So I walked through the streets of the city all night, trying to think what to do. In the morning I went to work as usual and remained at my office all day. You can ask my assistant — he'll tell you I was there. I worked until seven in the evening, and then I couldn't stand the pressure of my thoughts any more. On an impulse I ran to the phone and reported Farley's murder."

Morgan's fiancée spoke again, this time to Detective Flint. "I suppose that just for the record you'll want to know where I was last night?"

"No, that's not necessary," said Flint. And turning

to the wiry little man, he said with disgust, "Mr. Wadsworth, your story of how you learned of Farley Morgan's murder is obviously a lie. I certainly hope you didn't think that I'd be fooled by it!"

HOW DID DETECTIVE ARTEMUS FLINT KNOW THAT MR. WADSWORTH HAD LIED?

If Morgan had been murdered more than 21 hours previously, as Mr. Wadsworth claimed he had, blood would not still be dripping "profusely" from his head and forming "an ever-widening blotch on the rug." He would have stopped bleeding by then. The murder must have been quite recent, or the blood would already have coagulated.

The Case of . . .

The Broken Bowl

"I hate to bother you, Mr. Flint," Dora Wyatt said. "But I'm in real trouble — over something I didn't do!"

"What's your problem?" asked the kindly detective.

"I work as a domestic for Mrs. Miller. Last Wednesday I was cleaning her house. In her living room I noticed that she had a beautiful new green china bowl, with many tiny pictures painted on it."

Mrs. Wyatt continued. "I picked it up to dust it. Just then Mrs. Miller's daughter Lynn came running into the room. Two of her young friends were chasing her. They stopped when they saw me. I said, "Goodness, you startled me. I nearly dropped this new bowl." They ran to Lynn's room. I put the bowl back on the shelf. Then I started to clean the kitchen."

"Later, Mrs. Miller came home. Lynn ran to the door shouting, 'Mommy, Dora broke the new green bowl. I saw her do it.' I tried to defend myself, but Mrs. Miller would only listen to Lynn. And Lynn was lying."

"I'll speak to her," said Artemus Flint.

Flint visited the Millers. He asked Lynn how she knew the bowl had been broken.

"After my friends left," said the girl, "I was

13

bored. So I decided to spy on Dora. I saw her leave the kitchen and go back to the living room. She picked up the bowl. Then she sneezed and she dropped it. It broke into a few big pieces. She picked them up just as my mother was coming in the front door. I ran to the door to greet my mother. I didn't want to tell her what had happened. I hoped Dora would tell her, but I saw she wasn't going to. So I told Mother. I took her into the kitchen, and I reached under the sink, behind the pipes, where Dora had hidden the pieces, wrapped in newspaper. Dora said I was lying, but Mother knows I don't tell lies."

"There's always a first time," said Flint. *"You're lying now!"*

HOW DID DETECTIVE ARTEMUS FLINT KNOW THAT LYNN WAS LYING?

Lynn knew where the pieces of the broken bowl were hidden. Yet according to her story, she went to greet her mother just as Dora was picking up the pieces. If this were true, she wouldn't have seen them hidden and wouldn't have known where to find them.

The Case of . . .

The Businessman's Bribe

"I am accusing Commissioner Tinker, the city's Commissioner of Business Operations, of having accepted a $500 bribe, Detective Flint," John De Mar announced. "I want you to see that he is brought to justice."

"Whom do you suspect of having bribed him, Mr. De Mar?" the famous detective inquired.

"I don't suspect, I *know*," Mr. De Mar said heatedly. "It was Grover Matthews, President of the Bargains Galore Store, and my chief competitor. I happen to be the owner of Nifty Thrifty Shop."

"Ah yes," said Flint. "You and Grover Matthews own the two largest budget shops in town. What do you claim that Matthews wanted the Commissioner to do — why did he bribe him?"

"Matthews bribed the Commissioner to get him to accuse my store of cheating the public. It's not true, of course. And my honesty will be proved in the end. But even being *accused* of cheating our customers will ruin our reputation. It will probably even drive us out of business!"

"Why don't you start from the beginning," suggested Flint. "Tell me the whole story."

"This morning, Commissioner Tinker came to my

15

store. I spoke with him in my private office. He told me that charges of cheating the public had been made against my store and that his department would have to investigate them. Naturally this means publicity in the newspapers — just the thing that would ruin me. He hardly listened when I told him the charges were false. Right after he left the store, I went out for lunch. I saw Commissioner Tinker, and with him was Grover Matthews. I saw Matthews pass a wad of bills to him. Then the Commissioner got into a cab and left. I lost sight of Matthews."

"That's quite a story," remarked Artemus Flint, puffing on his pipe.

"Why don't you call in Grover Matthews and see what he has to say," challenged De Mar. "Of course, he'll probably deny the whole thing."

"I'm sure he will," Flint said. And then, looking De Mar squarely in the eye, he added, *Because your story is a lie!*"

HOW DID DETECTIVE ARTEMUS FLINT KNOW THAT JOHN DE MAR WAS LYING?

Mr. De Mar accused Commissioner Tinker of having accepted a $500 bribe. If, as De Mar said, he had seen Matthews "pass a wad of bills to the Commissioner," De Mar would not have known the amount of the bribe.

The Case of . . .

The Cobra Gang

"Many clergymen work with street gangs," Reverend Andrews told Detective Artemus Flint. "But the Cobras are more dangerous than any gang I've heard of. I'm afraid some harm will come to Reverend Lacey. He's been working with the Cobras for a month now."

"Trying to help those kids go straight is a good thing," said Flint. "Maybe he can use my help."

The next day Flint visited Reverend Lacey in the basement where the Cobras held their meetings. None of the gang members seemed to be around.

"Actually, I could use your help, Mr. Flint," the priest told him. "A gas station near here was held up the other night. The thief wore a Cobra ring. The boys won't tell me who did it. If I go to the police, I'm afraid they'll haul in the whole gang. Then these boys will never trust me. They'll go from bad to worse. So I want to find out by myself who did the holdup."

"I'll see if I can help you find out," said Flint. "Let me look over the gas station and talk to its owner. Then I'll come back to talk to the Cobras."

"Why don't you come next Thursday?" Reverend Lacey invited. "The Cobras will all be here then for an important meeting." Flint agreed.

On Wednesday, Flint received the following letter in the mail:

Dear Detective Flint,

Don't bother to come Thursday. I found out it was a member of the Majestics, and not a Cobra, who held up the gas station. I knew God would help me find the truth, and he did.

Yours truly,
Reverend John Lacey

Flint grabbed his coat and ran outside. "I hope Reverend Lacey hasn't been hurt," he thought. "Because it's obvious that *he didn't write that letter!*"

HOW DID DETECTIVE ARTEMUS FLINT KNOW?

A clergyman using "he" to refer to God would certainly have capitalized the "H."

The Case of . . .

The Cruising Phonies

"It's always interesting to talk to people on a cruise, don't you think so, Mr. Flint? One meets so many different people, and so many interesting ones. Some are old and some are young. Some are privileged and some are self-made. Some — "

"Some are real and some are phonies," interrupted Flint. He was sitting on the ship's deck, warmly wrapped in a blanket lest a chill wind get at him, chatting happily with the old fellow beside him, a gentleman named Hammers.

"Of course when they're away from home, some people like to make themselves seem more important than they actually are," responded Hammers. "But do you really think it's possible to tell who's for real and who's a phony?"

"Not only is it possible," said Flint, "it's easy. All you have to do is listen carefully to what people say about themselves. Let's have lunch together now. Afterward, I'll tell you which of our table companions are phonies."

The two dined at a table for six. As was the ship's ritual, initiated by the social director, each of the guests in turn introduced and told a little about himself.

"I'm retired now, but I used to be very important

19

in the FBI," an elderly gentleman began. "The public wouldn't know my name, of course, because in my line of work we must keep our identities a secret. But I used to be quite well-known around the White House. My children used to be invited to the birthday parties President Truman gave for his children, and often my wife and I were guests at formal state dinners for visiting dignitaries. Yes, I've led a rich full life, and I could tell some of today's young people a thing or two about adventure." He chuckled, and gave the floor to the exotic-looking woman to his left.

"I used to be an opera singer, before I lost my voice. I've sung Butterfly in *Madame Butterfly* and many other important roles, but my most thunderous acclaim came when I sang the part of Mimi in *La Boheme*. But unfortunately I'm past my prime now. I'm just a has-been." Her lunch companions assured her that this was certainly not the case, as the next speaker, a lady by the name of Mrs. De Vries, began introducing herself.

"I'm a high school English teacher. I teach courses in American literature and in journalism, as well as the general English classes."

"Who are your favorite American authors?" asked Mr. Hammers.

"Twain, of course, is the finest," replied Mrs. De Vries, "but I also enjoy Hawthorne, Dickens, and Poe. I'm an avid reader. One can get so much vicarious pleasure from books, and there's always so much more to learn!"

After Mr. Hammers and Artemus Flint had introduced themselves, they heard from the final dinner guest, a gentleman by the name of Hughes.

"I'm a doctor," he explained. "My specialty is ophthalmology, the care and treatment of the intestines. But in addition I'm also very interested in geriatrics. You might say studying the aging process and elderly people is sort of my hobby. A strange hobby, but a very interesting and worthwhile one."

Hammers rushed through his meal fairly bursting with curiosity. Once outside, he pulled Flint aside.

"Well," he challenged the famous detective. "If there are any phonies among them, I certainly can't tell. Can you?"

"It's child's play," said Flint. "I can tell you that three of those people are phonies. And I can tell you *which* three are phonies — and how I know!"

WHICH OF THE FOUR OTHER LUNCHEON COMPANIONS WERE PHONIES? HOW DID DETECTIVE ARTEMUS FLINT KNOW?

The first companion and the last two companions were phonies. The elderly gentleman referred to "the birthday parties President Truman gave for his children." President Truman had only *one child,* his daughter Margaret. Mrs. De Vries included Dickens among her favorite American authors. Dickens was British. "Doctor" Hughes described ophthalmology as the care and treatment of the intestines. That is wrong. It concerns the care and treatment of the eyes.

The Case of . . .

The Deceptive "Dancer"

"Thank you, miss. Next dancer, please."

"Stop! Stop!" shouted a man as he ran into the darkened theater. "Don't anybody move. Stay right where you are. Turn on the lights."

"Would you mind telling me, please, what all this excitement is about?" asked Director Gerald Hartman. "We're in the middle of an audition to choose dancers for our play, and we're running late as it is. What's so important that you must interrupt the audition?"

"The theater's box office has been robbed!" gasped the man. "I'm the cashier. I thought I had locked the box office when I went to lunch. But when I came back I saw a woman leaving the box office. I shouted at her and tried to block her way. She couldn't escape, so she ran the only way she could — into the theater. I found the entire week's receipts missing from the cash register. The thief is in here somewhere, I know. She's mingled with the others. We've got to find the deceptive 'dancer.' "

"Maybe I can help," offered Detective Artemus Flint, who had been invited to the audition by Hartman. "I noticed five young ladies came in late — well after the others."

He looked at the first, a hard-looking woman with dyed red hair, a tight blue sweater and skirt, some-

22

thing white tied around her foot, and a cigarette in her hand.

"Why were you late?" asked Flint.

"I stopped at the doctor's office before coming here. We had an argument. You see, I had sprained my ankle and he had treated it. He told me I could definitely have the bandage removed today, so I could audition for the play. But when I stopped in at his office on my way to the theater today, he changed his mind. I felt terrible, but I decided to come to the audition anyway, just to see if those who got the parts could dance as well as I can."

Flint moved on to the second latecomer, a painfully thin woman in a short skirt and black stockings.

"I was late because my little boy was sick and I couldn't get anyone to stay with him," she explained. "My neighbor, who usually looks after him, is visiting her mother in the South, and all the high school girls were in school. Finally I remembered Mr. Devita on the first floor, who's retired. He agreed to look after my son while I came to audition. I rushed here right away."

The third woman explained that she had gotten onto the wrong train and had gone a long distance out of the way before realizing her error. "When I got off the train, I had to wait about twenty minutes before the next one came along, and it was a local. If only the city had better signs and more frequent trains — "

"Thank you," Flint interrupted. "And you?" he turned to the next latecomer. "How can you explain your lateness?"

"I overslept. I was up very late last night. It's as simple as that. And don't think I'm not fighting mad about it. I'm a better dancer than any of these 'chorus girls.' I'm a ballerina. I've studied ballet for years with the best teachers. I know all the traditional ballet steps, and all the Italian words we use to name them. So it's really maddening that now I probably won't get a chance to audition at all."

The last woman began her explanation without even having been asked. "I thought the audition began at twelve thirty. It was only as I left the house and looked at the audition notice to check the audition address, that I accidentally noticed the audition time — eleven thirty. I've been on the stage for a long time, and never before have I made such a mistake." As she started naming the plays she had been in, Artemus Flint turned to Hartman.

"You'd better call the police," he whispered. "Tell them that when they arrive, one woman will be waiting here with me — the deceptive 'dancer'!"

WHO WAS THE DECEPTIVE 'DANCER'? HOW DID DETECTIVE ARTEMUS FLINT KNOW?

The fourth latecomer questioned by Flint was the deceptive 'dancer.' She claimed to know all the traditional ballet steps and the Italian words we use for their names. Flint knew that French, not Italian, names are used.

The Case of . . .

Farmer Foster

Sitting in the cozy farmhouse, gazing out at cows in the field and relaxing in a comfortable old armchair, Flint felt content. Now it was time for him to hear from Amy Foster about the problem that had brought him to her farm.

"A man named Jebson wants to buy out all the farms in the area and consolidate them into one big farm — his," she explained. "But I won't sell. I'm happy living and working here."

Amy Foster had the look of a woman who worked outdoors: She was a farmer. She and her husband Bob owned their small farm, which didn't earn enough to support the family. To supplement their income, Bob had taken a factory job in a neighboring town. Amy ran the farm.

"I've heard talk around the village — nasty, threatening talk," she told Flint. "It makes me fear that Jebson will try to sabotage my farm in some way, in order to force me to sell. I believe I've got good reason for my fears, but honestly, Mr. Flint, it's gotten so that I'm suspicious of everyone."

Flint knew that Amy Foster was not easily ruffled, and he understood her present concern.

"Of whom are you suspicious?" asked Flint.

"Well, for example, the other day the mailman was

supposedly sick, and a man came who claimed to be his replacement. I began talking with him, and we got onto the subject of stamps. When I mentioned that I was an avid stamp collector, he told me he would come back soon and bring me a new stamp just printed — with a picture of the present King of France on it. 'An exceptionally pretty stamp,' he said. Is he for real? Or does he just want an excuse to nose around my farm?"

She continued without a pause. "And then there was the hunter who was prowling around. He said he was hunting for red foxes. Then he started telling me about foxes — claiming that generally in the United States a significant part of the fox's diet consists of field mice! Sounds preposterous to me! Was he a real hunter, or was he prowling about my farm for the purpose of sabotage?"

"And listen to this, Mr. Flint," she went on excitedly. "A man came to the door yesterday. He claimed Bob had mentioned to a friend of his that we have a rat problem in our barn — which we do. He recommended that we get a dog — a terrier. He said cats are fine, but he's always preferred terriers for catching rats. He told me the name of a kennel where I could get one. 'Get a good ratter,' he said, 'and your problems will be over.' He's going to have a look around the barn one of these days, he said, to see how his advice has helped. Another ridiculous-sounding piece of information!"

"Am I getting paranoid?" Amy Foster asked at last. "Or are these men planning to sabotage my farm?"

"You have good cause for alarm, Mrs. Foster," Flint

said. "Not all those men are what they pretend to be. They weren't all telling the truth. I'll tell you whom to suspect — of misrepresentation of identity and perhaps of intention to sabotage your farm!"

WHO DID FLINT THINK HAD LIED AND MIGHT INTEND SABOTAGE? WHY?

Flint thought the first man was the would-be saboteur. There is no present King of France. The other two men had given accurate information.

The Case of . . .

The Four Suitors

"It's a troubling problem, Flint," Mrs. McAdoo told her good friend as she poured a second cup of tea for him. "My daughter Betty is currently going out with four different men: Jerry, Jeff, Hank, and Phil.. I've met them all and they seem nice enough. But one can never tell, can one?" She cocked her head to one side.

"What are you getting at, Lulu?" Flint asked, looking up momentarily from his second helping of hot apple pie.

"There are rumors and allusions about, but no one tells me anything directly. My friend Winnie said the other day that someone who had know Betty's brown-haired suitor in France told her on excellent authority that he had been convicted of smuggling there, but had escaped from jail. But you see how complicated it is: Phil, Jerry, and Jeff all have brown hair!

"Winnie also said that the police know all about him, and extradition proceedings are about to begin," Mrs. McAdoo added.

"Why don't you speak to Betty directly about this?" Flint asked.

"Oh, Flint, don't you see? She'd think I was one of those mothers who pry and snoop. And I'm not. I'm really not. I'm just looking out for her welfare. Just to spite me, she'd probably take up with the one who's a criminal. It seems to be a commonly known fact among my friends that *one* of Betty's suitors is a criminal." Stirring her tea nervously before she had put sugar in it, she continued talking.

"What really troubles me is this, Flint. Betty tells me that she's fallen deeply in love with one of her young men and that they plan to announce their wedding plans soon. I'm so worried that her future husband and the smuggler will turn out to be one and the same! Oh dear, and I shall not be able to find out in time to save her from the heartbreak!"

"Of course you shall, my dear Lulu," Flint said, patting her hand reassuringly. "Artemus Flint is here." Flint took it that that was explanation enough.

Mrs. McAdoo stared thoughtfully down at her teaspoon. "My friends tell me that I've never spoken with the criminal, just greeted him on his way in and out, that sort of thing. It's just so impossible to *know*, Flint. I'd be flabbergasted if Phil were the criminal. He's led such a sheltered life — never traveled abroad, never lived away from home, always taken good care of his widowed mother. He still lives with her, you know."

"Tell me whatever else you know about the four young men," requested Flint.

"Well, Jerry's a dear! He's got dimples and green eyes and he really listens when you talk to him. No one has ever been so interested in the story of my operation last year as he was. Really a dear, dear boy," concluded Mrs. McAdoo.

"Betty's friend Marsha knows who Betty's true love

is. She'd never violate a confidence, of course," — here Mrs. McAdoo's rosy blush indicated that she had learned this from personal experience — "but she did tell me that he has brown eyes."

Then came another thought: "I wonder whether Betty's true love got the raise he was going to ask for. She thinks he deserves it. He's always worked so hard at the office, she says — he's done so despite his personal problems: Since his mother's death, he's the one who looks after three younger brothers."

"Lulu, your tea is getting cold," Flint reminded her gently.

But she was miles away. "Jeff is a farmer," she murmured, more to herself than to Flint. "At least if Betty should marry him, she'd always have enough to eat." Mrs. McAdoo was momentarily content. Then she remembered the problem. "But what if he's the smuggler? Of course, she'd have enough to eat with him too, but I mean an escaped smuggler! One simply cannot have an escaped smuggler in the family, can one?" The blue eyes looked at Flint in wonderment.

"Lulu, you do have such a charmingly scatterbrained way of giving information. I've managed to put together what you have told me. You want to know who Betty's true love is? You wonder whether he is the same person as the criminal? I'll tell you!"

WHO IS BETTY'S TRUE LOVE? IS HE THE SAME PERSON AS THE CRIMINAL? WHO IS THE CRIMINAL?

The criminal has brown hair, which HANK doesn't. Mrs. McAdoo had spoken with JERRY at length, though not with the criminal. PHIL has never traveled abroad, and the smuggler was convicted in France. Therefore, *JEFF must be the criminal.*

JERRY has green eyes and Betty's true love has brown eyes. PHIL lives with his mother, while Betty's true love's mother is dead. Betty's true love has "always worked so hard at the office"; JEFF is a farmer. So who does that leave? *HANK, true love.*

The Case of . . .

The History Mystery

Seven cash prizes of $1000 each were to be awarded to the college students who had written the best paper in the field of American history. One student from each of 50 colleges was waiting in the hotel ballroom to hear the awards announced. Pete Manley, a friend of Flint's, was in the running, so Flint attended the ceremony.

Before it began, Flint moved among the crowd of outstanding history students. He heard snatches of conversation.

". . . which is why I chose to study President Willard Fillmore, instead of one of the more well-known American presidents," said a sandy-haired young man to his date.

"I wrote on the nineteenth amendment — which gave women the right to vote — because there's so much concern with women's rights today," said a tall muscular man.

"In *Poor Richard's Almanac*, Benjamin Franklin wrote a lot of wise advice. I find it still good today. I learned a lot from . . ." The speaker was a serious-looking young woman.

". . . and if it hadn't been for the case of *Marbury v. Madison*, the Supreme Court wouldn't have such far-ranging power. Without judicial review . . ." Flint looked at the speaker, a freckle-faced man.

The meeting began. One of the cash prizes was awarded to Robin Hailey. The person who went up to accept it was one of those whose conversation Flint had heard before the meeting. As the person rose to accept the $1000, Flint jumped up and shouted, "Stop! That's not Robin Hailey. *That's an impostor!*"

WHICH PERSON WENT UP TO RECEIVE THE AWARD? HOW DID ARTEMUS FLINT KNOW THAT THAT PERSON WAS AN IMPOSTOR?

The sandy-haired young man went up to receive the award. That young man said he was studying President *Willard* Fillmore. President Fillmore's first name was not Willard, but *Millard*, as the real Robin Hailey would have known.

33

The Case of . . .

The Humorous Hijackers

When Flint saw the couple who had been assigned the seats next to him on the plane, he knew he would know no peace on this trip.

"We're the MacGregors, Ida and Joe — I'm Joe, but they call me 'Mac.'" Flint shook hands.

"Say, do you know how long this flight lasts? I wonder if we'll arrive on time. Will they serve dinner on the plane?" Mac kept up a steady stream of questions. When he stopped, his wife started in.

"Mac owns a roller coaster," Ida said to Flint. "Whenever anyone asks him how's business, he always says —"

"It has its ups and downs," Mac finished.

They both laughed heartily at the old joke. Flint managed a faint smile.

"No, seriously," Ida said, "Mac's in the dry-cleaning business. He owns two places. Business is good — otherwise we'd be home instead of flying off into the wild blue yonder. You're probably wondering what I do," Ida finished.

Nothing could have been further from Flint's mind.

"Knit," said Ida.

"What?" asked Flint, in spite of himself.

"Knit. I run a knitting store."

Mac took his cue and said, "Don't worry, I won't let her pull the wool over your eyes."

More laughter.

Flint picked up his newspaper, hoping to silence the pair. He was not on a pleasure trip — he was on the plane to prevent a hijacking. It was believed that this plane was going to be hijacked. Flint's job was to see that this didn't happen.

His neighbors rattled on. He peered over the top of his newspaper at the other passengers. Perhaps the hijacker would give himself away.

". . . and she wanted to buy enough yellow yarn for the whole dress at one time. 'That's silly,' I told her. 'Buy just part of the yarn now. You can always come back for more. And if we run out, we'll order more for you.' That's the kind of shop I run. My customers trust me. They know that . . ."

Flint tuned Ida out and went back to scrutinizing his fellow passengers.

". . . so when the new dry cleaner opened up down the block from my Adams Street place," Mac was saying, "we thought we'd lose business. But no — our customers stayed with us. Inside of three months, the competition folded. I never could understand it. Just bad luck, I guess — for them."

Flint closed his eyes and let his mind wander. Then something came back to him — something he'd once been told. He raced to the cabin in the front of the plane.

"The woman sitting next to me probably is an impostor," he announced. "I suggest she be watched closely. I wouldn't be surprised if she and the man

35

with her aren't innocent passengers — but *would-be hijackers!*"

WHY DID DETECTIVE ARTEMUS FLINT THINK THAT IDA WAS PROBABLY AN IMPOSTOR?

Ida said she ran a knitting shop. She also said she encouraged a customer to buy just a little yarn now, come back for more, and "if we run out, we'll order more for you." As anyone who *really* ran a knitting shop would have known, knitters should buy all of their yarn for one project at once to be sure that it all comes *from the same dye lot* — that is, yarn that was dyed at the same time. Otherwise, in ordering more, one will get yarn from a different dye lot — dyed at a later time and likely to be of a slightly different shade.

The Case of . . .

The Ideal Idol

"It's an ideal opportunity, Flint," said Bart Colly, the crude, flashy, self-made millionaire. "I'm through with investing in Wall Street. The stock market is too unreliable. Instead, I've decided to take up artifacts."

"Artifacts?" asked Flint. Somehow the idea of broken pieces of pottery, sculpture, and daily utensils dug up from centuries ago did not fit in with his impression of Colly's interests.

"Yes, ancient artifacts," Colly replied, scratching his nose and revealing the diamond pinkie ring on his left hand and the ruby cuff link on the wrist. "I've had what I consider to be a great offer. It's a private offer, through an antiquities dealer named Leonard Castle, whom a friend of mine introduced me to. Castle told me that because I'm 'a man of distinction' — *his* words — and because I'm just beginning my collection — he's expecting a lot more business from me in the future — he's giving me an opportunity to buy an ancient artifact that recently came into the hands of a dealer in Israel. It was dug up in the Negev and is thought to be a fertility idol from before the time of Abraham. An early people believed that praying to this idol would yield them fertile fields and a good harvest. Such an idol is, of course, very valuable, and its value would grow even greater with time." He licked his lips at the thought.

"What do you want me to do for you, Mr. Colly?" Flint asked, anxious to get to the point.

"Come with me to meet Castle. I want your opinion of him and of the deal before I go through with it," Colly requested.

A short time later the two men were in Leonard Castle's living room. Castle was clearly nervous. His fingers twisted his hair and loose threads on his jacket, unbent paper clips, and fidgeted with almost everything possible. His short jerky movements and chain-smoking confirmed the impression of nervousness.

"I've asked you two gentlemen to my home instead of my gallery because this is a very special, private undertaking." As he spoke, his eyes darted furtively from Flint's face to Colly's and back again. "This fertility idol is a real find — I'd keep it myself if I could afford to. It's rather small, measuring only eight inches in height, but it's the only one of its kind that's ever been found, and so is of great worth." From the gleam his words brought to Colly's eyes, he knew he'd said the right thing.

"How does Mr. Colly know that it's all on the up-and-up, that it's legal, authentic, and so on?" Flint asked coolly.

"Of *course* you'll want proof," Castle replied. "Here," — he reached into a desk drawer and pulled out a yellowed piece of parchment, "is an old scroll which helps to authenticate the pottery. The scroll is more recent of course than the idol, but it does explain that such figures were known to have been produced by these people at that time. And I have here a letter from the dealer in Tel Aviv who first acquainted me with the existence of this fertility idol. The letter is written in Hebrew, of course. Does either of you gentlemen read Hebrew?"

The two shook their heads.

"Then I'll translate it for you." He took a folded sheet out of an envelope that was on his desk, opened it, and began reading, muttering softly to himself what to Flint were incomprehensible sounds. Castle's eyes moved slowly from his left to right as he read each line and then darted quickly back to his left again to begin a new line. "I have to read Hebrew slowly and say the words to myself as I read," he explained. "It's a difficult language."

Flint and Colly watched him as he read, waiting patiently for his translation to begin.

"Now I'm ready," Castle said at last. "I just wanted to refresh my memory so that I could get it exactly right for you. In his letter, the dealer in Tel Aviv assures me that he has government permission to export the fertility idol. He encloses two letters — also in Hebrew, unfortunately, since you can't read it — from world famous anthropologists vouching for the authenticity of the idol."

"Well, I guess that clinches it, Flint," Colly said, rubbing his hands together with satisfaction. "This idol is an ideal first piece for my collection. I'm going to buy it."

"I wouldn't advise it, Mr. Colly," Flint said. The millionaire's hands stopped in mid-rub and his mouth sagged open. "The devil finds work for *idle* hands," Flint said, "and clearly the devil has directed Mr. Castle in this matter. *The whole deal is a fake!*"

HOW DID DETECTIVE ARTEMUS FLINT KNOW THAT MR. CASTLE'S DEAL WAS A FAKE?

When Castle read the "Hebrew" letter, his eyes moved from his left to right as he read each line. Flint knew that Hebrew is read from right to left.

The Case of . . .

The Libertyville Murder

"It's sure nice that you called us when you were passing through Libertyville this evening, Cousin Artemus," said Flint's relative as he escorted him through the town's quiet streets.

Noticing Flint glancing at his watch, Cousin Fred went on, "Yup, just past six o'clock and already the whole town's shut down tight. That's what it's like in a factory town like this. Stores aren't open late but one night of the week, and that's the day after payday, when they don't close til 9 P.M."

Sitting at the dinner table with Fred's wife Polly and their two children, James and Jo Ann, Flint helped himself to a generous second helping of mashed potatoes, and asked, "What do people do for excitement around here? Doesn't anything interesting ever happen?"

"There was a murder last week," piped up James. "Tell 'im about that, Pa!"

"You tell him, son, since you seem to take such an interest in it," countered the father.

"Well, it's like this, Cousin Artemus," began James, fairly bursting with pride at having been chosen to be the one to relay the grisly news.

"Last Thursday at 8 P.M. a man named Wendell

41

Belong was stabbed to death in the middle of the local park. He was stabbed several times through the chest. He managed to drag himself along the ground a few feet, and then he died. The motive is clear: robbery. Thursday is payday at the factory, and Belong was a foreman there. But no one knows who could've done it!" He paused to let this sink in.

"But surely there are some suspects?" questioned Flint.

"Everyone thinks it was Mr. Bradley, but he says he was out shopping," interjected Jo Ann.

"Let *me* tell it!" James shushed his sister. "If it wasn't Mr. Bradley, then it must have been Mr. Winters or Mr. Peterson, most folks think. But they've got alibis too. Mr. Winters claims he went for a moonlight swim in the pond, and that other folks saw him there at the time of the murder. Mr. Peterson says he was puttering around with his car in front of his house, and that his neighbors saw him there. All three suspects seem to be telling the truth — but only one could have stabbed Wendell Belong — or perhaps it was someone else altogether."

"Some people say it was done by a tramp just passin' through town," interjected Cousin Fred. "I'm rather inclined to that theory m'self. Don't see how it could've been one of our local boys."

"It can — and it was," stated Artemus Flint, pounding on the table. "And I know *which* one it was too!"

WHO HAD COMMITTED THE LIBERTYVILLE MURDER? HOW DID DETECTIVE ARTEMUS FLINT KNOW?

Mr. Bradley had committed the Libertyville murder. He claimed to have been out shopping at the time of the murder. But at 8 P.M. on Thursday (payday) night, the stores were closed. They were open late only the night *after* payday, or *Friday night.*

The Case of . . .

The Long-Lost Niece

"I've asked you to come here today to help me decide which of three young women is my niece," Miss Elsie Angell told Detective Artemus Flint. "You see, my sister Louise and her husband moved to Switzerland shortly after their marriage. They had a child named Denise. Several years later, my sister died. Her husband stopped writing to me. He raised the child himself. Last year I received word that he died. I have been trying to find my niece ever since. I've even put ads in the newspaper."

Flint asked, "Why are you so eager to find your niece?"

"She is my only living relative. I want to get to know her. When I die, she will get a lot of money."

Flint spoke to the first young woman.

"You must believe that I am the real Denise Angell," she told Flint. "Ever since Papa died I've been all alone in the world. When I found out about Aunt Elsie, I was so happy! I hope she'll let me stay with her."

Then Flint met the second young woman.

"I am from the Spanish-speaking part of Switzerland," she explained. "Daddy worked in a bank there. Every night my mother would tell me bedtime stor-

44

ies about America and Aunt Elsie. I've always wanted to come here."

The third young woman told Flint, "If you only knew how happy I am to meet my aunt! My father was away most of the time — he was a seaman in the merchant marine. How often I stood on the pier in our village in Switzerland, watching his ship go out to sea! I felt so lonely then! I was raised by strangers. They didn't care what happened to me. But at last I've found a person who does care — Aunt Elsie."

Flint returned to Elsie Angell.

"Well," said Miss Angell, "which one of those women is my niece?"

"I'm afraid that *none* of them is your niece," said Flint. *"They are all imposters!"*

HOW DID DETECTIVE ARTEMUS FLINT KNOW?

The first young woman claimed to be "Denise Angell." Miss Elsie Angell's sister's daughter's name would not have been Angell.

The second young woman claimed to be from the Spanish-speaking part of Switzerland. There is none.

The third young woman said her father had been a seaman in the merchant marine, and she claimed to have often stood on the pier in her Swiss village watching his ship go out to sea. Switzerland is an inland nation.

45

The Case of . . .

Mandy Lynn's Murder

Detective Artemus Flint was sleepy. He had lain awake most of the preceding night. Something had been bothering him, a case he couldn't solve. The details kept repeating themselves in his mind.

There was Butch Randall, a pained expression on his pudgy face, asking Flint, "How can you think I'd do it? I loved Mandy Lynn. She was all I had."

There was Slicker Fox, hair greased down, saying in oily tones, "Mandy Lynn was an attractive woman. Sure, it hurt my pride when she tossed me aside for that big dumb Randall. But it was her loss, not mine. I knew there were other fish in the sea."

There was Mrs. Cramwinkel, Mandy Lynn's deaf old landlady, sobbing as she looked down at the dead girl and wondering aloud at the same time what the publicity would do to her "respectable boarding-house."

There was Stuart Cramwinkel, her stepson, a weak, fearful, selfish character as far as Flint could judge, a boy a few years younger than Mandy Lynn who'd obviously had a crush on her and been harshly thrust aside by her.

And finally, there was Mandy Lynn — dead. Flint could see the body in his mind's eye. The delicate features, the cheap flashy clothes — and the stab wounds that had brought her to her end.

Sitting in his chair, Flint knew that something had kept him awake last night, a fact he couldn't place, something that didn't fit in. He got up now and began pacing the floor, hoping that the elusive tidbit would somehow come to him.

He reviewed the facts of the case: Mandy Lynn Wheeler, 20, restaurant cashier, dead of stab wounds. Body found in her room at 801 East Seventh Street. Found by her landlady who heard moans, sent stepson for police. With police, Flint interviewed Mandy Lynn's current and former boyfriends. Mandy Lynn had no family, no close friends.

Confronted by Butch Randall, Stuart Cramwinkel remembered having seen Randall leave the house immediately after the murder, coming down the steps as he went to get the police.

Who had murdered Mandy Lynn? And why didn't the facts fit into place? Flint couldn't face the prospect of another sleepless night. He *had* to solve the case — now. Returning to his chair, he closed his eyes and let the pictures flit through his mind's eye once again.

"Aha!" he said aloud a few minutes later. "I've got it. I know why the facts didn't fit into place. And I think I know who murdered Mandy Lynn."

WHO DID DETECTIVE ARTEMUS FLINT THINK HAD MURDERED MANDY LYNN? WHY DID HE THINK SO?

Flint thought Mrs. Cramwinkel and/or Stuart Cramwinkel had murdered Mandy Lynn. Mrs. Cramwinkel had "heard moans" and sent her stepson for the police. But Mrs. Cramwinkel was deaf. Flint believed that she had made up the story to protect herself or her guilty stepson — and that she had sent him for the police to further suggest his or her own innocence.

48

The Case of . . .

The Maximillian J. Ferrar Affair

The telephone rang.

"Artemus Flint, detective, here."

"Flint? This is Maximillian J. Ferrar."

Flint, like everyone else, recognized the name of the famous industrialist. His voice took on a slightly awed, more respectful tone.

"Yes, Mr. Ferrar. How can I help you?"

"You can come right over here to my office and protect me — keep them from getting me."

"Them? I'm afraid — "

"The kidnappers!" shouted Ferrar angrily. "Or abductors! Or whatever you call them! They're out to steal me! Or hijack me! Or — "

"Calm yourself, Mr. Ferrar," urged Flint, "and tell me what this is all about."

"I received a note this morning," said a somewhat less hysterical Mr. Ferrar. "It was made up of words and letters clipped from newspapers and pasted together. It said that I'm going to be kidnapped and held for ransom. The note threatens that — "

Through the receiver, Flint heard the other man's

phone fall, then some moans, a few rushed footsteps, and then a click as the phone was hung up.

Flint's course of action was clear. Moments later he was speeding to the Ferrar building, fortunately located quite near his own office, taking the elevator up to the 29th floor, knocking on the heavy wooden door, and facing a middle-aged woman on whose desk was a sign reading "Cara de la Vie."

"Are you the private secretary of Maximillian J. Ferrar?" Flint asked her.

"Yes, that's right," replied the woman, clearly wary of the nervous, sweating little man before her.

"I've got to go into Mr. Ferrar's office right away!" exploded Flint. "I'm afraid that something terrible has happened to him!"

"Don't be ridiculous," said the secretary, smothering a yawn. "Mr. Ferrar is perfectly all right. He's in his office now, and he gave me strict orders to let absolutely no one in. He's not to be disturbed at all now."

"But don't you see, this is a matter of life and death!" thundered Flint, lunging toward the door. But the secretary was ahead of him.

"*No one* goes in," she said in steely tones, blocking his way. "I've been private secretary to Maximillian J. Ferrar for 20 years, and I *never* disobey his orders."

Flint decided to try another approach.

"All right," he said calmly. "I'll take your word for it that Mr. Ferrar is well and in his office. Perhaps you can take a message for him."

"Certainly," replied the secretary sweetly, returning to her desk and picking up a pen.

"Tell Mr. Ferrar that Detective Artemus Flint was here to see him but that he was not — "

"Wait a minute! Not so fast!" interrupted the woman, who had begun writing the message down in a neat script.

Flint chose this moment to rush to the door to Ferrar's office, open it, and plunge in before the secretary could run around her desk.

Ferrar was nowhere to be seen. A few papers were scattered on the floor, and the private exit door from Mr. Ferrar's office was closed.

Taking in the situation at once, Flint went to Ferrar's phone and called the police. "Maximillian J. Ferrar has been kidnapped from his office," he told them. "If you come to the Ferrar building right away, *you can catch an accomplice of the kidnappers.*"

WHAT DID FLINT MEAN? WHY DID HE THINK SO?

getaway, taking Ferrar with them.

provide the abductors with needed time to make their

an imposter, posted at the door of Ferrar's office to

she couldn't, Flint thought that she must have been

shorthand without asking Flint to slow down. Since

tainly be able to write down a simple message in

a wealthy industrialist for 20 years, she would cer-

kidnappers. If she really had been private secretary to

Ferrar's secretary was really an accomplice of the

Flint thought the woman who identified herself as

The Case of . . .

The Misguided

Millionaire

"I need your help, Mr. Flint," said a voice breathlessly. "I'm afraid I'm going to be murdered."

Flint looked up as a tall man with dark hair and frightened eyes sat down in his office.

"Suppose you just relax a moment and tell me what this is all about," Flint advised the man kindly.

"I'm Roland Crisp," the visitor explained. "I'm due to inherit over a million dollars on my thirty-fifth birthday, which is next week. If I'm not alive on my thirty-fifth birthday, the money goes to my cousin, an unprincipled scoundrel named Pete De Champ. He would stop at nothing — even murder — to get the fortune."

That explains the man's frightened eyes, thought Flint.

"How can I help?" the detective asked.

"If my cousin decides to have me murdered, he'll have a perfect opportunity next week. Three days before my birthday, I'm planning to go on a trip to the northern woods, to photograph animals in their natural surroundings. I'll need a guide. I'm meeting with several possible guides this afternoon, and I want you to be with me. It's possible that my cousin will try to arrange for the guide to murder me in the woods. Maybe you can help me decide which guide not to hire."

Flint agreed to the plan, and found himself sitting in Crisp's living room as the first man entered to be interviewed.

"I've been guiding people through the northern woods for fifteen years now, son," a shaggy-haired old man assured them. "Know my way around better than you know your own face. You tell me what you want to see, I'll take you to it. I know parts of that woods that few people have ever seen — places where there are so many animals you won't know where to point your camera first."

The second candidate was a stern-looking man with a heavy accent and an air of professional competence. "You must understand the life cycle of the woods to be a good guide, and I do. I studied science in my student days, and I have lived most of my life in or near woods. I have a feeling for all living things. I can teach you, so your photographs will reflect this feeling, this concern for life."

When he left, a third man came in — one with bad teeth and a ruddy complexion. "We have a great deal of fun when I take a group through the woods," he said. "It's exhilarating. Why, I remember the last group I took through the woods, not more than four weeks ago. After a long day of hard hiking, we roasted game over the campfire. Then we all settled down for the night in our sleeping bags. Those people told me afterwards how beautiful it was for them city folks to sleep out under the stars, listening to songbirds, smelling the clean cool air, and feeling themselves surrounded by nature. You can have the same experience, mister, if you'll hire me as your guide."

After the door had closed behind him, Flint turned to Crisp and said, "You were right. One of the men we just interviewed is not a real guide. *That man might be the potential murderer you're afraid of.*"

WHICH MAN WAS NOT A REAL GUIDE? HOW DID DETECTIVE ARTEMUS FLINT KNOW?

The third man was not a real guide. He described the group as listening to the songbirds at night. In general, birds do not sing at night.

The Case of . . .

The Misled Musician

"There's no doubt about it," thought Flint as he stuffed the last morsel of cheesecake into his mouth and washed it down with hot chocolate, "eating is one of the supreme pleasures of life. Without it my vacation would have been a washout. Quite literally, too. When you come to the mountains with the intention of taking long walks in the brisk autumn sunshine, and every day begins with fog and ends with rain, there's little to do but remain in the nice warm hotel restaurant and eat. Lovely!"

"Do you mind if I join you?" Flint heard a voice interrupting his reverie. "All the tables seem to be occupied."

Flint indicated that the man might indeed occupy the place across from him. He surveyed his companion, a man in his early forties, with a sensitive face, patient eyes, a receding hairline, and a prominent birthmark on his right cheek.

A musician, I'd wager, thought Flint. Or a writer.

"Too bad I left my piano at home," said the man. "One needs something to do *indoors* in this weather." He laughed at his own little joke.

Right the first time, thought Flint. A musician.

"What's your line of work?" asked the man chattily.

"I'm a detective."

This interested the man greatly. His eyebrows rose and his Adam's apple bobbed.

"No kidding! You know, there's something I've been wondering about, an incident that took place last week. A problem I haven't been able to solve. It's been bothering me ever since. I wonder if you could help me."

Flint glanced outside. It was pouring, and the heavy gray clouds told him it would continue to do so for some time. "Why not?" he asked. "What's the problem?"

"I give private piano lessons," the man began. "Most students love the lessons, but a few are forced by their parents to take piano lessons, and they dislike them. They never practice, and they'd do anything to avoid taking the lessons.

"One Thursday evening I arrived at the home of such a student, Wes Kulligan, only to be told at the door by his younger sister that Wes was sick and couldn't take his piano lesson. When I inquired as to the exact nature of Wes's problem, the girl indicated the stomach. I asked to speak to her parents, but was told that she and her brother were home alone."

Flint ordered reinforcements — another hot chocolate, and this time a piece of raspberry pie to go with it — with whipped cream on top. Then he turned his attention back to his companion, who continued his narration.

"The next night I was at the home of Marshall Clamp, another piano student of mine. Marshall doesn't like studying the piano any more than Wes does, and he and Wes dislike each other cordially. They go to school together, and they seem always to be

56

getting into fights over one thing or another. This particular Friday night, I happened to mention Wes's illness to Marshall. 'Last night?' he asked me. 'But that can't be.' Why not? I asked. 'I don't mean to rat on poor old Wes,' he replied — which of course was exactly what he *did* mean to do — 'but I saw him outside last night, at about eight o'clock. That's when he has his piano lesson, isn't it?' he asked innocently. 'Where did you see him?' I asked. 'In the alley between Jefferson and Meredith Avenues. It was just before the storm began. I was rushing home from my friend's house. I took the short cut through the alley. There are no lights there, so I couldn't see very much. I could make out that someone was coming toward me on a bike. I heard thunder and then I saw a flash of lightning a moment later. By the lightning I could see Wes's face.'

"You can well understand my problem," the musician finished. "I don't want to accuse Wes of having pretended to be at home sick when he wasn't even at home. But I don't want to accuse Marshall of lying either. Which boy should I believe?"

"I don't mean to rat on poor old Marshall," Artemus Flint said, shoveling in a healthy chunk of raspberry pie, "but Marshall's the rat. He's the liar."

HOW DID DETECTIVE ARTEMUS FLINT KNOW THAT MARSHALL HAD LIED?

Marshall had lied when he said, "I heard thunder and then I saw a flash of lightning a moment later." Flint knew that the lightning would have been visible *before* the thunder was heard, not after. Light travels much faster than sound.

The Case of . . .

Mr. Blitz's Bribe

Rodney Harrow walked into the U.S. Customs Office.

"I have read that the Customs officials are trying to stop the smuggling of dope into the United States," he announced. "So I feel it's my duty to help you. I want to report a smuggler."

"Who is he?" asked the Customs officer.

"A Mr. Andrew Blitz from New York City. He was smuggling hashish."

"How do you know that Mr. Blitz is a smuggler?" the officer asked.

"I flew back to this country from overseas last night," Mr. Harrow explained. "Mr. Blitz was sitting next to me on the plane. We started talking. That's how I know his name. He's very rich. He says he is a salesman.

"He was ahead of me when we went through Customs," Harrow continued. "I am certain I saw him slip three bills to the Customs agent. The agent let him pass. He didn't check his luggage."

"There are always a few weak people everywhere who will take bribes," the Customs official sighed. "We try to weed them out of our department, though. The great majority of our agents are honest. Maybe you just *think* you saw the agent accept a bribe."

"No," Harrow replied. "I'm sure of it. I even overheard Mr. Blitz talking to a friend afterward. A short, gray-haired guy. We were all waiting for cabs. Mr. Blitz was saying, 'And it only cost me $100 to bribe the agent. Pretty cheap, eh? And that hash will bring us a fortune!' When I heard that, I knew I had to report him."

"I have made a note of all that you have told me, Mr. Harrow," the Customs officer said. "I'll take care of the matter. Thank you for coming in."

Then the Customs officer phoned Detective Artemus Flint to ask him to find Andrew Blitz. He repeated to Flint the whole story.

Flint said, "You don't want Mr. Blitz. He didn't do anything wrong. *Mr. Harrow's story is a lie!*"

HOW DID ARTEMUS FLINT KNOW THAT HARROW'S STORY WAS A LIE?

Harrow said Blitz had slipped three bills to the Customs agent. Then he said he overheard Blitz say it only cost him $100 to bribe the agent. No three bills total $100.

The Case of . . .

Mrs. Waltham's Party

When Mrs. Waltham gave one of her lavish parties, she liked to invite many different types of people. There were always a lot of rich people, her friends. They came with furs, jewels, and money. But she usually invited some college professors, artists, scientists, writers, and other scholars or experts. Variety made things interesting, Mrs. Waltham felt.

Detective Artemus Flint was attending his first party at Mrs. Waltham's house. There was a guard at the door, and he asked to see everyone's invitation. Mrs. Waltham wanted to make certain that no thief could get in and rob her guests.

Flint found himself sitting at a table with Professor Kirk, a famous zoologist who studied fish, Dr. Walker, a well-known brain surgeon, Charles Sedgwick, a detective story writer, and several of Mrs. Waltham's wealthy friends.

They were talking about how difficult it was to find good employees nowadays.

"The people who clean the operating rooms do a terrible job," said the doctor. "And the rest of the hospital staff has to be watched all the time. Otherwise, they forget to do something important."

"I've just had a problem with my assistant," Professor Kirk said. "One day while I was out he fed the wrong kind of food to some of my most expensive fish. When I got back, I found them all dead at the bottom of the tank. I fired the young man at once, of course."

"My secretary misspells words all the time," said Mr. Sedgwick. "He spells 'murder' as 'merder,' 'weapon,' as 'weppin,' and 'police' as 'polease.' But I can't afford to pay a high salary, so I'm lucky to have any secretary at all."

Mrs. Shaw, one of Mrs. Waltham's friends, said, "One of our maids, Gertrude, has broken two lamps and a very expensive ashtray in the last month. But what can I do? She's a lovely person, and she's been with me for years. I couldn't think of firing her."

Flint slipped away from the table and went up to the guard at the door.

"There's someone here who is a fake," Flint whispered to him. He pointed to one of the guests. "Watch that person," he cautioned. "That person probably is a thief!"

TO WHOM DID DETECTIVE ARTEMUS FLINT POINT? HOW DID HE KNOW?

Flint pointed to Professor Kirk. Dead fish do not sink to the bottom; they float on top, as anyone who studied fish surely would have known.

The Case of . . .

The Murder on the 7:36

Detective Artemus Flint took in the whole picture: neat gray wool suit, immaculate white cotton gloves, small hat, sensible shoes, perfect grooming. Such a person, he thought, would not be likely to have an illogical mind. Precision, he thought, was the word that would best describe Miss Peters.

"Good morning, Miss Peters," he greeted her. "I am Detective Artemus Flint. We've invited you here — "

"You haven't invited me here," she interrupted, "you've herded me here — along with the other passengers. As if we were all guilty. As soon as the train pulled in to the station, we were all taken by the police directly to your office, to be questioned one by one. I demand to know what's behind all this. I had scheduled an important business meeting this morning, and it cannot begin without me."

"I'm deeply sorry, Miss Peters," said Flint comfortingly. "But murder isn't a matter to be taken lightly."

"Murder!" exclaimed Miss Peters.

"Yes, murder. We've asked you to come for questioning about the murder that took place this morning on the 7:36 commuter train from Woodstone."

"So that's what all the commotion was about," she said. "I heard someone scream, and I looked up from my newspaper to see a crowd gathered around a man seated a few seats ahead of me. Since I couldn't see what was going on. I went back to my paper. I have no information for you, no clues, no ideas."

"You read the newspaper throughout the trip?" asked Flint.

"That's right. I bought it at the station before I got on the train, and read it until the train arrived. Then I left it on the train. It's my business to keep well-informed about the news."

"Yes," said Flint, "of course. You see, a man was found stabbed to death on this morning's train. There were fingerprints on the knife, and we hope to match them with those of one of the passengers."

"Well, they couldn't be mine. You see, I kept my gloves on for the entire trip."

Flint said, "One of the passengers indicated that you had been sitting next to the man who was later found murdered, but had changed your seat."

"I had been sitting several seats up — now that I think of it, that *was* the seat where the crowd gathered. The man next to me was alive and well. In fact, he was too well — kept talking and talking, until I finally had to move so I could read in peace."

"Perhaps that's so," Flint said slowly. "But I'm afraid we'll have to keep you here for further questioning about the murder on the 7:36."

"Why, it's perfectly preposterous to think that I had anything to do with it," shouted Miss Peters indignantly.

"If that's so," said Flint, *"then why did you lie to me?"*

HOW DID DETECTIVE ARTEMUS FLINT KNOW THAT MISS PETERS HAD LIED?

If Miss Peters had kept her gloves on throughout the trip and had bought and read the newspaper, her white cotton gloves would have been stained from the newspaper ink. Since they were immaculate, Flint knew she had lied.

The Case of . . .

The Murdered Miser

"I received another one of those anonymous letters today, Flint," shouted a panicky Wilfred O'Toole. "The writer threatens to kill me. You've got to come over and tell me what to do!"

By the time Detective Artemus Flint arrived, Wilfred O'Toole was dead. Upon breaking down his door, Flint found him slumped over his desk, a knife in his back.

Flint had had enough dealings with the mean-spirited miser to know who his enemies were. Several people had a motive for killing him, Flint realized. There were the two men whom O'Toole had referred to as "Van den Hoek and his crazy uncle," whose business O'Toole had ruined. There was his niece Vickery, whom O'Toole had threatened to cut out of his will unless she stopped seeing a certain favorite but impoverished boyfriend. There was his sister-in-law Barbara, who lived shabbily on O'Toole's meager allowance, but who would benefit handsomely from the old miser's will. And there was Lloyd Creasy, a former employee of O'Toole's, and the father of seven children. After years of loyal service to O'Toole, Creasy had been fired for making a costly mistake. O'Toole, in his anger over

65

money lost, had made it impossible for Creasy to find decent work again.

Flint phoned Creasy first.

"Hello, Mr. Creasy? This is Detective Artemus Flint. I'm calling on a matter involving Mr. Wilfred O'Toole. I want — "

"Wilfred O'Toole!" sputtered Creasy. "That snake, that no-good so-and-so! Don't mention his name to me! He ruined me — ruined my career, ruined my reputation, ruined my life. The world is better off without him!" A click told Flint that Creasy had hung up the phone.

Mr. Van den Hoek was equally honest, but more polite to Flint: "I consider the name of O'Toole a curse and utter it as infrequently as possible. My uncle and I had a thriving business until your client's underhanded methods forced us into bankruptcy. O'Toole is totally lacking in ethical or human qualities. Good-bye, Mr. Flint."

From Barbara O'Toole, Flint received a curt reply: "Please tell my brother-in-law that I am doing my best to manage on the allowance he gives me, and that in no way can he accuse me of being extravagant."

Vickery Marrow at least feigned a liking for her uncle. "We don't always see eye to eye," she told Flint, "but he has my best interests at heart. I know that."

Flint made one last phone call — to the police. "I want to report the murder of Wilfred O'Toole. I have a strong suspicion that he was murdered by — "

WHOM DID FLINT SUSPECT? WHY?

Flint suspected Lloyd Creasy. Creasy said of O'Toole, "The world is better off without him!" If he hadn't known O'Toole was dead he would have said, "The world would be better off without him." If he knew he was dead, then he must have had some connection with the murder.

The Case of . . .

The Nervous Niece

"Money was of the utmost importance to my Uncle Carl, and he hoarded it. But for some reason I liked him, Mr. Flint," said Alice Eustace.

"And you say you tried to telephone your uncle but received no answer?" queried Flint.

"I've been trying for a week now. Frankly, I'm worried. What if something has happened to him? He was a likely target, you know. He lived alone in a fleabag. His room was as dingy as they come. But sewn into his mattress he had thousands of dollars in cash. Yes, believe it or not — sewn into his mattress!"

"Have you or your cousins ever tried to persuade him to use a bank?" asked the detective.

"Have we! Nearly every time we visited. But he thought banks weren't secure enough."

"And how often *did* you visit, Miss Eustace?" asked Flint.

"Very often. My cousins and I could use the money, while the old man had no use for it at all. We hoped to talk him out of some of it. But he wouldn't part with a penny. No matter how good the reason," she added somewhat bitterly.

"Let's go over to your uncle's room and see if

68

we can get in. Maybe we'll learn something there," suggested Flint.

The Savoy Hotel was as seedy as Miss Eustace had intimated, thought Flint as the two entered the lobby together. Approaching the desk clerk, Flint explained who they were and why they wanted to be admitted to Carl Eustace's room. After a whispered conference with someone in the back room, the desk clerk accompanied them to a room at the end of a smelly second floor corridor. Using his passkey, he opened the door and preceded them into the room.

A bare yellow light bulb was burning, warming the many flies and moths that hovered around it. It illuminated a horrifying scene. The mattress had been ripped apart, and mattress stuffing was scattered about. There was blood over everything. And in the center of the room lay the dead body of Carl Eustace with multiple stab wounds.

Alice Eustace turned away in horror. The desk clerk's bored expression changed to one of astonished revulsion. And Flint's steely eyes narrowed. He pointed a long finger at Alice Eustace, and said in measured tones:

"*You! You're* responsible for this! You played a part in this! You *knew* your uncle was to be murdered. Perhaps you caused him to be murdered. Or perhaps you murdered him yourself!"

HOW DID DETECTIVE ARTEMUS FLINT KNOW THAT ALICE EUSTACE HAD BEEN INVOLVED IN HER UNCLE CARL'S MURDER?

While claiming that she was worried about her uncle's safety, Alice Eustace referred to her uncle from the very beginning *in the past tense.* Clearly she knew of — and perhaps played a part in — her uncle's death.

The Case of . . .

The Pickpocket at the Party

Someone screamed, "I've been robbed! My money — it's gone!" Then other people joined with cries of "My wallet's been stolen!" "Police!" "Help — we've all been robbed!"

It was just what Detective Artemus Flint had feared. In recent months, wealthy guests at a number of nightclub parties had been robbed by a very clever pickpocket. None of the victims had realized what was happening — until it was too late and the thief had fled.

So for the Permingtons' party, the police surrounded the nightclub and mingled with the guests. And as an added precaution, Detective Artemus Flint himself was invited.

And now the worst had happened.

Flint took charge. Immediately, people began rushing up to him.

"I was about to leave," said one well-dressed man. "I was talking with the coat-check man about movies. He was telling me about a good one he had seen last night — and then I heard the screams. I looked for my wallet — it was gone!"

A pale man spoke up. "I was dancing with a very

witty young lady. She had told me about her trip to New York last summer, and I was going to ask her whether she had seen the new World Trade Center. Then someone screamed. The young lady turned white when she realized her wallet had been stolen from her purse. Fortunately, the thief didn't get my wallet."

"One of the waiters spilled coffee on my dress," exclaimed a silver-haired lady. "I was so upset! Do you think he might have planned to take my handbag while I was distracted? Oh dear!"

"I thought the food was superb — especially the dessert," a round-faced man remarked. "I was in the kitchen getting the recipe from the chef. He had just written, 'Add lemon juice, flour, and sugar, and simmer over a high flame' — when I heard someone scream. I rushed back into the ballroom, and learned what had happened."

It was Flint's turn to speak. "The thief must still be on the premises. The police have had the nightclub surrounded, so no one could have left." He paused and looked around. "The pickpocket is still here — and I think I know who it is!"

WHO DID DETECTIVE ARTEMUS FLINT THINK WAS THE PICKPOCKET AT THE PARTY? WHY?

Flint thought the round-faced man was the pickpocket. If he had really been speaking with the chef, he would not have been told to "simmer over a high flame." To simmer is to cook at less than a boil; to cook over a high flame would result in boiling.

The Case of . . .

Sammy the Show-off

Flint rarely went to the beach — especially on such unusually cold days as today. It was a cold day in an unusually cold summer for New York. Flint was thoroughly miserable. He hated getting sand in his eyes, hated having seaweed wrap around his toes, hated to expose his poor milky shoulders to the elements. But here he was at the ocean's shore, and all because his sister, whom he was visiting in New York, had a persuasive way about her.

"Please, Artemus," she had begged, "for your nephew Clem's sake, if not for mine. Clem insists on going to the beach at Long Island Sound with a group of his young school friends, but I won't hear of their going without some sensible adult going along to guide them. And since I can't, I thought . . ."

So Flint had obligingly gone to the beach to "sensibly guide" Clem and his friends. The few of Clem's friends he'd heard about he didn't like. There was Alice, a girl who giggled a lot, and Steve, a boy who cleaned his fingernails with his jackknife. There were Ted and Debbie, who were "going together," and then there was Sammy the Show-off, sometimes called Sammy the Storyteller, who always made himself the center of attention, even if he had to fabricate stories to do it. He annoyed Clem like mad.

Feeling sorry for subjecting himself to the tortures of wind, cold, and sand, Flint left his blanket and walked to the refreshment stand. Finding that he could tolerate no more than one gulp of the orange drink he'd bought, he headed back to his blanket.

There he was accosted by Clem and his friends all talking excitedly at once. Words assailed his ears. "Sammy went swimming—" "—been gone a long time," "—not been seen—" "—we're all so worried," "What should we do?" Flint lost no time in piecing together the story. When he had, he headed immediately over to the nearest lifeguard.

"A boy is missing," he reported. "Sammy Karlstone, fourteen years old, tall, brown hair. Last seen swimming in the ocean about fifteen minutes ago. Not seen since." Sammy's friends pointed to the area where they had seen Sammy dive into a wave—the last they had seen of him.

The lifeguard whipped into action. He sounded an alarm, summoned aid, and started launching lifeboats. As he was about to hop into a boat himself, a figure was seen swimming toward the shore. It was Sammy. The lifeguard sprang into the water, and with a few powerful strokes reached the boy and helped him onto the beach.

Lying on the sand, his chest heaving, surrounded by a circle of his friends, lifeguards, curious observers, and Detective Artemus Flint, Sammy haltingly told his story.

"A shark," he gasped. "I was attacked by a shark. I

74

was swimming out pretty far. Where it's deep and cold. Sharks like cold water. This one was really mean-looking. It almost got me. After I dove through a wave and gashed my shoulder on a rock, I surfaced and I saw the shark in front of me. It bumped against me several times, as if trying to decide where to bite first. While kicking its head away with my foot, I managed to use my arms to pull myself closer to shore. I kept kicking the shark's head and swimming until I got into shallower water, where the shark wouldn't follow me. I was never so scared in my life. I thought for sure I'd be that shark's dinner!" He could talk no longer. He lay in the center of the crowd, panting.

The crowd was thrilled. Someone spoke of calling a newspaper reporter. Someone else treated Sammy's badly bleeding shoulder. Clem scowled. Once again, people were making a fuss over Sammy.

At last Sammy had caught his breath. He stood up and grinned. "That was quite an experience, wasn't it?" he asked his audience.

"It would have been," said Flint, feeling rather ridiculous with his stomach hanging out of his faded red bathing trunks as the crowd turned to look at him. "As it is, you've needlessly endangered other lives by occupying the lifeguards and the rescue equipment. For your sake, I hope you didn't *mean* to alarm everyone."

The boy's mouth fell open.

"Yes," continued Flint, "it *would* have been a remarkable experience. If it had taken place. *But it never did!*"

HOW DID DETECTIVE ARTEMUS FLINT
KNOW THAT THE EXPERIENCE SAMMY HAD
DESCRIBED HAD NEVER TAKEN PLACE?

Flint knew that sharks rarely appear in the waters
off the northeastern United States, and that when
they do, it is only in unusually warm weather. This
was an unusually cold day in an unusually cold
summer. Furthermore, if there *had* been a shark —
an extreme unlikelihood — it would have smelled
the blood from Sammy's gashed shoulder and attacked
him. It is highly unlikely that he would have gotten
away unharmed.

The Case of . . .

Stella Tilson's Ghost

The steps of the "haunted house" creaked under the weight of Detective Artemus Flint. Without hesitation, he opened the door, went in, and found his way to a bedroom. This was where he was to spend the night.

It was all because Charlie Zyke, Ray Mirado, and Jake Barton said he'd be too scared to do it. "You know that old Tilson house?" Jake had asked him yesterday. "They say it's haunted by Stella Tilson's ghost."

"Humph. Ridiculous," Flint had replied, puffing on his cigar.

"No, it's not," Charlie had told him. "Stella Tilson was strangled in that house on New Year's Eve just two years ago. Her body was taken away, and it was never found."

Nor was the killer, Flint remembered. There had been no witnesses. Stella had lived alone in the huge house after her family had died or moved away. Since it was far from any neighbors, no one had heard her cry out.

"They say," Ray had added, "that Stella's ghost will never rest until her killer is found. You don't believe in ghosts, Art? Then why don't you spend the night at the Tilson house, just to prove you're not chicken?"

And Flint had taken on the dare, so here he was. He sat on a rusty bed and a cloud of dust arose. He thought about the house and why he was here. "Aha!" he cried, the ghost of a smile flitting across his face. He jumped up, ran from the house, went quickly to a diner and called the police.

"Remember the Stella Tilson murder case?" he asked. "I've found a suspect. Either he knows who the murderer was, *or he murdered Stella Tilson himself!*"

WHOM DID DETECTIVE ARTEMUS FLINT SUSPECT? WHY?

Charlie Zyke mentioned that Stella Tilson had been strangled. Yet no one had been nearby at the time of the murder, and her body had never been found. He could have known that she had been strangled only if he had strangled her or knew the person who had.

The Case of . . .

Susan the Beachcomber

Detective Artemus Flint found high schooler Susan Lottingly walking along the beach. He fell into step beside the red-headed girl.

"It isn't just chance that brings me here, you know, Susan," Flint said. "It's my work."

"What's up? Somebody steal a sand crab?" joked Susan.

"It's serious," replied Flint sternly. "Last night someone sneaked into Mrs. Zeff your principal's office and stole the answers to the statewide history exam. The thief probably thought no one would notice, since the exam is two weeks away. He or she probably planned to copy down the answers and return the answer sheet before anyone knew it was gone."

Susan began twisting her long hair as Flint continued. "But this morning Mrs. Zeff discovered that the answer sheet had been stolen. She called the police. Officer Farber, who patrols the high school neighborhood at night, recalled that last night he had seen a tall girl with long red hair running about a block from the school. There aren't many students who fit that description. We're checking up on all of them. You're one."

"It's ridiculous to think that I stole those answers, Mr. Flint," Susan said. She stopped walking and turned. "I was here last night." She pointed to her small tent further down the beach close to the water. "That's where I slept last night. On that very spot, in my tent. I came out here yesterday afternoon about this time, pitched my tent there right away, and there it has stood and I haven't left since. I went to sleep early, spent the whole night in my tent, and got up at sunrise. It's been a beautiful, inspiring experience. Getting back to nature is my thing."

They wandered along the ocean's edge in silence for a few moments keeping well away from the water. Susan's bare feet kicked up the green seaweed that had been deposited by the tide. Then Susan said, "I don't know if I can make you understand, Mr. Flint. All you adults think success is so important. Good grades, good schools, good jobs. But that's not what I think. I think beauty is important: the sun, the water, the birds. I don't care enough about history to steal the exam answers."

"Maybe not, Susan, but you care about your friends. If you don't pass the history exam, you'll have to repeat history. That would be very embarrassing for someone who's an honor student in all her other courses. I'm afraid I'm going to have to bring you back with me for further questioning."

"You can't call me guilty because I'm a poor history student!" Susan said indignantly.

"I'm not," said Flint. "*I've got a far better reason for thinking you might be guilty.*"

WHY DID DETECTIVE ARTEMUS FLINT THINK SUSAN MIGHT BE GUILTY?

Flint knew that Susan could not be telling the truth. She alleged that the tent had not been moved for 24 hours. However, the beach on which she had pitched her tent was a tidal beach. The tide in that season went up beyond the tent, as evidenced by the still-living, *green* seaweed deposited further back than the tent by the tide. The high tide — which would have occurred at least once during the 24 hour period — would have flooded the tent and caused it to collapse.

The Case of . . .

The Unreal Rowboat

"So it seems they've picked George up at sea, Artemus, and he's on his way home now." George's wife Rita breathed a sigh of relief. "When I first got the telephone call yesterday telling me that my husband was alive and had been rescued, I was just wild with joy. After the children, you were the first person I called."

"I'm sorry I couldn't get here until today," said Flint. "I had to investigate three new cases: Steve Wintergreen's murder, Babs O'Donnell's suicide, and a case of smuggling — I had quite a busy time of it. But I came as soon as I could. Tell me what happened, Rita."

"Well, I don't really know very much, Artemus. Of course, you know that George was out to break some stupid record by travelling a great distance in a rowboat. Evidently he drifted off course and was lost. He was due to land nine weeks ago, but nobody had seen hide nor hair of him. Everyone tried to tell me that he'd probably been drowned, but I wouldn't believe it. You don't know George if you think he could be beaten by some water — even a whole ocean full of water."

"He's been at sea all this time?" asked an incredulous Flint.

"That's right. He had been adrift in the rowboat for nine weeks before he was picked up by a Japanese cargo ship. And he'll be here any minute!"

"Amazing! He'll undoubtedly have exciting adventures to tell about," commented Flint.

"Oh, I know!" Rita enthused. "Before he left he arranged for a magazine to print his story when he returned. There was even the possibility of a book contract, but that was really only an outside chance, only if something *really* interesting happened. But still, it was something we both had hoped for since it means a lot of money. And now, everything has turned out *better* than we could have hoped for! George will *certainly* get to write a book now — and we'll make a fortune!"

Moments later a tired, bearded, but healthy George arrived, and after the reporters and photographers had left, he finally had a chance to talk with his wife and with Flint.

"You should've seen the faces of the neighbors as I drove by with a police escort. Billy Pfifer just gaped. Steve Wintergreen's widow — I don't think you've ever met her, dear — walked into a lamppost. And old Mrs. Garrity started cheering."

"But I'll be glad when all the hoopla's over," he continued, "and things get back to normal. It'll take me forever to tell you the story of how I managed to survive all those weeks alone at sea."

"It'll take you forever to *invent* the story, you mean," interjected Flint. "You haven't been at sea all that time at all. Your story is a lie!"

HOW DID DETECTIVE ARTEMUS FLINT KNOW THAT GEORGE WAS LYING?

If George had been adrift at sea, he would not have known of Steve Wintergreen's murder. But when he referred to Wintergreen's wife as his "widow," George gave away the fact that he had actually been very close to home all along.

The Case of . . .

The Upside-Down Cakes

Detective Artemus Flint knocked on the cabin door. George Topper, unshaven and filthy, invited him in.

"It's a good life out here in the woods," Topper told him. "The last three days have been the happiest I've known. I haven't budged more than a few miles from the cabin — and I did that just to walk in the woods. I haven't heard another human voice until now. No contact with the outside world — no radio, television, mail, telephone — it's marvelous for a change. Give me the simple life anytime!"

"Let me give you some news from the outside world instead," said Flint. "Someone broke into the Pat-a-Cake Bakery. Nothing was taken, but the place was really messed up: glass counters smashed, whipped cream squirted all over, cakes thrown on the floor, refrigerators unplugged. A thorough job of vandalism."

"Sounds messy," Topper remarked.

"It was. I asked myself, Why would anyone do it? What could have been the motive? And then I remembered something."

"And what was that?" Topper asked, suddenly concentrating on a loose floorboard.

"Something I'd heard about. Last week, the police

tell me, you went into the Pat-a-Cake. You were hard to please, and I guess the salesman got impatient. So you became very nasty and called out insulting things about the baked goods. As I heard it, you said things like, 'Don't buy the cherry pie, folks. It's moldy,' 'The whipped cream is probably shaving cream,' and other such remarks. Finally, you were thrown out. You shouted back, 'You won't get away with this! You'll hear from me again!' Now *that's* what I'd call a motive," Flint concluded.

"Are you suggesting that *I* vandalized the Pat-a-Cake the night before last?" asked George, seemingly astonished. "Do you really think that that's the sort of obvious, heavy-handed revenge I'd take? No, Mr. Flint. I'd do something much more clever. That is, *if* I planned to 'get back' at the bakery. Which I don't. You're wrong this time, Flint. I'm innocent."

"Tell that to the police, George," snarled Flint. "*I* don't believe it."

WHY DIDN'T DETECTIVE ARTEMUS FLINT BELIEVE GEORGE TOPPER'S STORY?

Topper claimed he'd been at the cabin for three days, during which time he'd spoken to no one, heard neither radio nor television, and received no mail. Then how could he have known that the Pat-a-Cake Bakery had been vandalized "the night before last"?

The Case of . . .

The Vanished Van Gogh

When the police showed her a picture of Terry Fisk, Mrs. Benedict identified him at once. "Yes," she said, "he's the man who stole the Van Gogh painting from Mrs. Wheeler's home. I'm absolutely certain."

"Let's hear his story," Flint said.

Terry Fisk was brought in for questioning. The young man had a face and build that would be easy to remember, Flint noticed.

"Mrs. Wheeler's painting was stolen between ten and eleven last Saturday morning. Were you on Standish Street during that time?" Flint asked.

"Sure. I deliver laundry for the Moretski Brothers' Laundry and Cleaners. We have a lot of customers on Standish Street," answered the young man.

"Did you go into the Wheeler home?" Inspector Charles asked.

"No. When I brought the Wheelers' laundry and dry cleaning, no one was home. So I left their things on the back porch. Then I went away."

Flint asked Fisk to leave and Mrs. Benedict to come in.

"Saturday morning at ten I went to work in my greenhouse," she told them. "Working with plants is my hobby. My greenhouse is behind my home. I was in the greenhouse, surrounded by my plants. After a while I started to feel faint from all the carbon dioxide the plants were giving off. I had trouble breathing. I thought I'd pass out. I managed to stagger to the door, and I went outside. I stood in my backyard taking deep breaths to clear my head."

"Then what happened?" Flint asked.

"I saw that young man — Fisk — go to the Wheelers' back door. They're my next-door neighbors. He rang the bell a few times. When he realized that no one was home, he found the key under the mat and let himself in. A few minutes later, he left with the painting and drove off in the laundry truck. I was too stunned to realize what had happened until later. He had already disappeared with the painting by then."

"Why did you come to the police," Flint asked Mrs. Benedict, "when all you wanted to do was tell them *a lie?*"

HOW DID DETECTIVE ARTEMUS FLINT KNOW THAT MRS. BENEDICT WAS LYING?

Mrs. Benedict could not have felt faint "from all the carbon dioxide the plants were giving off."

Green plants are primarily producers of oxygen. Green plants are the source of most of the oxygen we breathe. Through the process of photosynthesis, green plants, using the energy of sunlight, manufacture carbohydrates from carbon dioxide and water. Oxygen is released during this process.

The Case of . . .

The Vase of Venus

Artemus Flint was a guest at the island home of multimillionaire Kirby J. Grant. The island, not far from the mainland, could be reached only by private boat.

"I know you appreciate ancient works of art, Art," Grant said to his friend as they sat at dinner. "That's why I wanted you to be with me when the Vase of Venus arrives."

"Tell me how you came to buy the Vase," Flint requested.

Grant said, "Last summer, I bought it from a man in Marrakesh. It was a highly secret deal. As you know, the Vase of Venus is one of the great art treasures of the world, and the dealer was afraid it would be stolen from him. I paid him in full. He agreed to have his representative, a man named Pol, deliver the Vase here tomorrow. I'm sending my yacht over to the mainland at eleven thirty in the morning to pick him up."

Just then the butler entered.

"A man named Pol is here to see you, sir."

"Pol! Here already?" said Grant. "Well don't just stand there. Show him in, show him in!"

The butler returned, followed by a slight man who was dripping wet from head to toe.

The Case of . . .

The Worried Witness

Flint went into the hospital and up to Miss Goldstein's room. A nurse was in the room, and as Flint entered, she said to Miss Goldstein, "Time to take your pulse." She pressed her thumb against the inside of Miss Goldstein's wrist, looked at her watch, and waited a short while. Then she rose, wrote something on the chart, and left.

The 90-year-old Miss Goldstein turned to Flint and said, "I've asked you here to prevent them from murdering me."

"Prevent *whom* from murdering you?" asked Flint.

"Paul Brian's friends. They know I saw the murder, and they want me dead."

"Time to take your temperature," said a second nurse, entering. She shook down the thermometer, put it in the old woman's mouth and said, "Be sure it's under your tongue." She went out, returned several minutes later, and took out and read the thermometer. She wrote something on the chart and left.

"Tell me what happened, from the beginning," said Flint with interest.

"Last week William Stevenson was stabbed to death in the alley behind my house. The police don't know who did it. But I do, because I happened to be